The Adventures
of
Ben the Mouse

Book One

Andy Coltart

 New Generation Publishing

To my children, Grace and Sam, without whom these stories would never have been told at bedtime as they grew up.

To Luca,

I hope you enjoy going on these adventures with Ben the mouse

Andy.

Contents

Acknowledgements

Firstly, to my friends John Winterton, Steve Brierley and Lizzy Biggs for all their hard work editing the words and artwork for my book.

Secondly, to Laura Levy, one of my art students, for providing the design for the duckling on page 60.

Finally, to the staff in my local Costa for the endless coffees they served me while I was writing and illustrating this book.

Ben the Mouse and the Magic Ring

Chapter 1

Let me introduce you to a little mouse called Ben. He is a very friendly little mouse. If you were to see lots of mice together you'd know which one was Ben straight away, because Ben always wears a red jumper with a letter B on the front. A Scottish hamster made the jumper for him as a birthday present, but I'll tell you more about him later on.

Ben lives in a hole in the wall of the Harwoods' kitchen. The Harwoods are an elderly couple living in Lichfield. They don't have children but they do have a very old, fat black cat called Hodge. Hodge spends most of his time sleeping on the sofa. He and Ben do their best to avoid each other. Ben is sure Hodge is too old and slow to catch him, but he doesn't want to put that to the test.

The Harwoods live in a little bungalow on the edge of town. It's a wonderful little home. It has an old longcase clock in the living room that rings out every 15 minutes, disturbing Hodge as he snoozes on the sofa. There are always interesting smells coming from the kitchen, as Mr Harwood loves to cook. If he has any cheese left over from cooking he will often leave some out for Ben. The bungalow is just down the road from a nearby farm. Our story will take us to the farm but first let's go inside the hole in the wall and see where Ben lives.

Ben's home is very cosy. Perfect for a little mouse to keep warm in on cold winter nights. It only has two rooms. One is his bedroom, with a soft feathery bed in one corner and a box in another in which Ben puts his jumper when he sleeps. Folded on his pillow is a small nightgown to help keep him warm at night.

The other room in Ben's home is a little bigger. It has a small table with three chairs – one for him and the other two for his two friends Louis, a field mouse and Haggis, the Scottish hamster. The rest of the room has a small sofa and a fireplace with pots and pans hanging above it. There is also a cabinet with shelves full of various things Ben has collected over the years. Inside the cabinet is where Ben keeps his hot chocolate powder and his cheese.

Chapter 2

Ben was woken this morning by a cold breeze blowing into his home from across the kitchen. Mr Harwood had opened the back door to let Hodge out into the garden. There was a light frost on the ground and the cat wasted no time running across the grass to avoid his paws getting cold.

Ben stretched out his little arms and pulled back the covers. It was time to get up and see what the day had in store. Once he'd put his jumper on he made his way through to the living room. The fire was still glowing from the night before, so he added some sticks to get it going for his morning drink. Now, most of us would enjoy a cup of tea and some toast for breakfast, but not Ben. His favourite breakfast was a warm cup of hot chocolate and a piece of cheese. The cheese had to be the sort with big holes in.

As he sat at the table he made plans for the day in his head. As Hodge was already gone he just needed the Harwoods to take their morning walk to Stowe Pool, a nearby reservoir. He could then safely make his way across the kitchen and use the cat flap to get out of the house. With his cheese and hot chocolate finished it was time to set off. Cautiously he made his way out of his mouse hole and across the kitchen, which was now deserted. Once he'd climbed through the cat flap he headed down the path and onto the road that leads to the nearby farm.

His best friend, Louis, was a field mouse and he lived in the corner of one of the farmer's fields. Sam, the farmer, and his wife, Megan, were both very kind people. They loved all the animals on their farm, including visitors like Ben. As Ben arrived Sam was busy moving the pigs out of the sty and into a field so he could clean up in there. Not a job *he'd* want to do, thought Ben.

Ben walked to the large field behind the farmhouse. He could see Megan at the kitchen window. She was probably cleaning up after breakfast. On entering the field he made his way along the edge to the far corner. There he found his friend in among the tall strands of grass. 'Morning, Louis,' he said. 'Morning, Ben,' came the squeaky reply from the little field mouse. 'So what's the plan for today?' said Louis. 'I thought we could explore the woods near the duck pond,' said Ben. 'Good idea,' said Louis, 'as long as we are out of there before it gets dark. That's when the owls like to get up and go looking for the likes of you and me!' 'Good point,' said Ben.

The two of them set off across the field. The quickest way to the woods, and the pond, was right through the middle of the field. As they approached the middle of the field a huge shadow was cast over them. They both looked high above their heads to see Mikey, the shire horse, standing in his usual spot. 'Hello, Mikey,' they both squeaked as loudly as they could. Mikey lowered his head, with his mane falling to one side. 'Hello, boys,' he said. 'And just where are you two off to on this cold morning?' 'The woods,' squeaked Louis. 'Be careful in there, you two,' said Mikey. 'That's no place for little mice, especially when it's dark.' 'We will,' said Ben, and with that they continued their walk through the long grass to the edge of the field.

Chapter 3

As they left the openness of the field they could see Mikey way behind them still standing there, eating some hay that Sam, the farmer, had put there for him. Ahead of them were hundreds of tall dark trees. The ground changed from long grass to muddy tracks with broken acorns, twigs and other things scattered along them.

'So where to now?' said Louis. 'Straight on,' said Ben confidently. They'd both agreed, on their way across the field, not to venture too far into the woods. They'd decided to stay close enough to the edge to always be able to see the field. As they wandered along they picked up acorns and threw them. 'This is fun!' said Louis. 'Just be careful where you're throwing that acorn!' said Ben, as one flew past his ear. 'What's that?' asked Louis, pointing ahead of them. 'I don't know,' replied Ben. 'Let's go and take a look.'

As they approached the strange shiny object, they could see it was round in shape. Louis went to pick it up. 'Careful,' said Ben. Louis pulled his hand back on hearing Ben's warning. 'What is it?' said Louis again. 'I think it's a ring. People wear them on their fingers. The Harwoods both have one,' said Ben. The two mice carefully moved the dirt from around the ring so that it lay in a small clearing. It was gold and glistening, even though there wasn't very much light shining on it. 'Wow,' said Louis, 'it's beautiful.'

Ben decided to pick it up. It was lighter than he expected. As he and Louis put their hands on the ring it started to glow. They wanted to let go but they couldn't! Next, the ring started to shake, making their arms move up and down. Without them realising it, the ring had lifted the two mice off the ground. Ben looked down. 'Oh, my!' he said, as he started to move round and round in a circle. 'We're spinning!' said Louis. They were turning faster and faster. So fast, in fact, that their ears were flapping. Their tails and feet were flying out behind them. The two mice squeaked as loudly as they could and as they did so a loud popping sound filled their ears and they came crashing down on the ground.

'Where are we?' asked Louis. 'Still in the woods, I think,' replied Ben. But there was no sign of the field and Mikey anymore. If it was the same woods they must be much further in than they were before. The pair looked around them. It seemed darker here. The trees were bigger, with more leaves and larger branches. 'I'm scared,' said Louis. 'You should be,' said a voice from above them in the tree. 'Who's there?' asked Ben, his voice trembling a little.

'Wilson,' came the voice from the tree. 'Who's Wilson?' asked Louis. At that moment a large brown and grey owl flew down and landed, with a thud, on the ground in front of them! The mice looked at each other, terrified and frozen to the spot. 'What are you two doing this far into the woods?' asked Wilson. 'We don't really know,' replied Ben with a frightened look on his face. Wilson was looking them up and down, clearly trying to decide whether to question them further or to have them for lunch. As a very wise owl, he decided to question them.

'You two don't need to look so worried. I'm not going to eat you. I'm just interested to know how you got here.' With a huge sigh of relief, Ben spoke: 'Well,' he said, 'we were at the edge of the woods playing when we came across a golden ring.' Wilson looked at them, intrigued. 'Go on,' he said. Ben continued: 'We didn't know what it was and when we picked it up it span us around and brought us here.' 'Hmm,' said Wilson. 'Let me see this ring of yours.' Ben stepped forward, very cautiously, and put the ring down in front of Wilson. The owl leant over to take a closer look. After a minute or two of poking the ring with his beak he stood back up. 'Well,' said Louis, 'what do you think?' Wilson paused before speaking, as if preparing to share his wisest thoughts. 'I'm sure you two have found the Willow's Ring,' he said. 'What's the Willow's Ring?' asked Ben. 'It's a golden ring with magic powers. It's made from the Golden Willow Tree, which has its own magic powers.' 'A magic tree!' said Louis, 'I've never heard of such a thing.' 'I'm not surprised,' said Wilson, 'for the tree has not been seen for hundreds of years. No one knows where it has gone.' Louis looked at Ben. 'So you're saying this tree can move,' said Ben. 'Oh, yes,' said Wilson. 'Just like you did when you held its ring. If I'm right, that ring will take you wherever you ask it to!' 'Wow!' said Ben and Louis together.

Chapter 4

'So,' said Wilson, 'what are you two going to do with this magic ring of yours?' Ben and Louis looked at each other. 'Have some amazing adventures!' said Ben with a smile on his face. 'Well,' said Wilson, 'I'll leave you to get started. Just one word of wisdom from a wise old owl. Make sure, wherever you go, to keep that ring safe. If you were ever to lose it you would be trapped wherever it had taken you.' 'Good advice,' said Louis. 'Thanks for your help, Wilson,' said Ben. 'My pleasure,' said Wilson as he took off like a rocket and flew back to his perch high in the branches of the tree above them.

'So,' said Louis, 'where shall we go first?' Ben thought for a moment, looking at the golden ring among the leaves on the ground. 'Scotland!' he said. 'Let's visit our friend Haggis the hamster!' 'That's a great idea. We've not seen him in so long,' said Louis. 'Well,' said Ben, 'are you ready to go?' 'Ready when you are,' replied Louis. The two mice stood round the magic ring. They leant over and picked it up. As they each placed both hands onto the ring it began to glow. But instead of squeaking loudly this time, Ben spoke clearly. 'Take us to Haggis!' he said. Their arms were shaking again as the ring glowed brightly. This time they felt their feet leave the ground and the ring begin to turn. 'We're spinning again!' said Louis. They were turning faster and faster – so fast their ears were flapping and their tails and feet were flying out behind them.

Then, just as before, with a loud 'pop', they came crashing down to the ground. But this time they knew what to expect, so they both landed on their feet still holding the ring. 'Where are we?' asked Ben. 'I'm not sure,' said Louis, 'it doesn't look like Haggis's castle.'

Suddenly a bright light appeared high above them. Then a loud Scottish woman's voice called out: 'Hamish, get in here right now, the pot is boiling! Time to put in the haggis.' 'Och aye, woman,' came a voice from the room next door. Ben and Louis grabbed the ring tightly and ran behind the kitchen bin. 'What's happened?' said Louis. 'The ring has taken us to Scotland and to a haggis. But it's a haggis that this man Hamish is cooking for his tea. It's not our friend,' said Ben. 'What are we going to do?' asked Louis, with a clear and audible panic in his voice. 'We are going to stay calm, and quiet,' replied Ben. He was used to being in kitchens and avoiding dangers, such as Hodge the cat. 'Let's just wait until they've finished and gone and we can try again with the ring,' said Ben. 'Maybe this time we should give it a bit more detail, like an address!' said Louis. 'Agreed!' said Ben.

The two mice waited quietly behind the kitchen

bin, while Hamish cooked his dinner. The only scary moment came when he used the bin to get rid of some packaging. 'Phew,' whispered Louis, 'I thought he was going to spot us then.' Finally the light went off and Hamish and his wife left the room. 'Right,' said Ben, 'let's get out of here.' The two mice placed both their hands onto the ring and as it glowed and started to shake Ben spoke clearly, saying: 'Take us to Haggis the hamster's castle at Loch Ness!' The mice rose from the floor, span round and with a loud 'pop' disappeared. The light came back on in the kitchen and Hamish said: 'What on earth was that wee popping sound?'

At exactly the same moment, Ben and Louis landed on their feet outside a huge castle by Loch Ness. 'Yes!' exclaimed Louis, 'We made it!' 'Yes indeed!' said Ben as he knocked on a tiny door in the wall of the castle.

Chapter 5

Slowly and with the smallest of creaks the castle door opened. Standing in the door was a fat little hamster wearing a green tartan kilt and a green jacket. 'What on earth, no, how on earth are you two here!' proclaimed Haggis in a loud Scottish accent. 'Are you going to invite us in?' said Louis. 'Och aye,' said Haggis, stepping aside to let them through. 'Come on in and make yourselves at home.'

Haggis always had a fire burning in the castle. It was the only way to keep warm. The two mice sat themselves down next to the fire. 'Cocoa, anyone?' asked Haggis. 'Yes please,' they both replied. They knew cocoa was Haggis's word for hot chocolate, which they both loved. Haggis reappeared a few minutes later with a tray. On it were three cups of cocoa and three slices of Scottish shortbread. As they all settled down to eat and drink Haggis asked: 'So, boys, how did you get yourselves so far north?'

Ben and Louis began to explain about their adventures. How Mikey, the shire horse, had warned them not to go too far into the woods. How they'd found the ring and been transported to the darkest part of the woods. How they'd come face to face with Wilson, the wise owl. How they'd made it to Scotland, but had ended up in Hamish's kitchen. Then finally how they had arrived at the castle.

'And all of this because of a magic ring!' said Haggis, in complete amazement. 'Let's see it, then.' Ben placed it on the table in front of Haggis. 'Don't touch it with both hands at the same time!' said Louis. 'Why not?' asked Haggis. 'Because that's how the magic starts,' said Ben. 'It's taken us three goes to get it right, so we don't want to suddenly lose you before you know how to get home.' 'Aye, good point,' said Haggis.

After a close study of the ring Haggis asked if they knew any more about it. So they told him everything that Wilson the wise owl had said about the Golden Willow Tree. 'Wouldn't it be amazing to find that tree,' said Haggis. 'What for?' said Louis. 'I don't know,' said Haggis; 'maybe it has other secrets apart from this ring!' 'True,' said Ben, 'but for now we have the ring and the possibility of lots of adventures.' 'Would you like a wee adventure without the ring first?' asked Haggis. The two mice sat up: 'Yes, of course we would!' said Ben. 'Then follow me, boys,' said Haggis, and with that he stood up from his chair and headed for the door.

Ben and Louis followed. 'Where is he taking us?' asked Louis. They marched out of the castle and along a muddy track that led down a gentle slope towards the loch. 'Keep up, boys,' said Haggis, marching on ahead. Ben and Louis almost had to sprint just to keep up with him. Finally Haggis stopped. 'Here we are,' he said. 'There's nothing here!' said Louis. The three of them were now standing at the water's edge. The loch stretched for miles – so far, in fact, you couldn't see its end. All around, the mountains soared high into the sky. Some even disappeared into the clouds above. 'Why are we here?' asked Ben.

Haggis pulled a strange-looking horn from his pocket. 'For this,' he said, blowing into the horn. The horn made a strange eerie sound, like the one you get as bagpipes are warming up before they start playing properly. The two mice watched, confused as to what this noise meant and what their friend was up to. Then all of a sudden, with no warning at all, the water in this great loch started to stir.

Suddenly the surface broke and from its depths rose an enormous dragon-like creature, green and covered in scales. It had two small horns, little ears and large eyes. Its mouth was huge, with large shining teeth, and it had two big nostrils on its nose. About halfway down its back were what looked like wings folded in against its body. It had a long tail, the end of which was popping out of the water behind it.

'Meet Nessie!' exclaimed Haggis, with a sense of pride in his voice. The two mice were on the ground. They'd fallen over in shock. As they stood up Nessie glided through the loch to the water's edge and stopped with her nose just in front of Ben, Louis and

Haggis. 'Hello, beautiful,' said Haggis. Nessie smiled. 'Beautiful!' shouted Louis, as if his friend had clearly not seen the monster before them. Nessie frowned and looked straight at Louis, which made him step back a little and keep his mouth shut.

'She's amazing,' said Ben. 'How on earth did you come to meet her and have that horn to call her with?' 'Well,' said Haggis, 'your ring isn't the only magical thing around here. Look across the loch at that man fishing. He's not even noticed Nessie is here.' 'How's that possible?' asked Louis, 'She's huge!' Nessie frowned at him again. Louis quickly went quiet. 'Aye,' said Haggis, 'but she's also magical and people can't see her. Only animals can.'

'OK,' said Ben, 'but that still doesn't explain how you found the horn to call her with.' 'True,' said Haggis. 'That was the strangest thing, if I'm honest. I woke up one night and could hear singing coming from the loch. So I came down here in the dark and began to realise the singing was under the water. And then, there it was, lying on the shore. Right where we are now. That little horn. When I blew it, it made that strange noise. But when I put the end in the water and blow, it sounds like the singing I heard. That's when she first appeared and we've been getting to know each other ever since.'

Chapter 6

'That's incredible,' said Ben. 'Yes, it is,' said Louis. 'Aye,' said Haggis. They all stood admiring the magnificence of Nessie.

Then Haggis spoke. 'Would you boys like to see the loch, Nessie style?' There was an excitement in his voice, probably because he knew what was coming next. 'Sounds fun!' said Ben. 'Erm, OK,' said Louis, a little more cautiously. Haggis turned to Nessie and smiled. 'You up for giving a tour?' he said. Nessie lifted her huge head and nodded. As she did, she splashed water all over them. After wiping his face,

Haggis said: 'Follow me, boys.'

Nessie had opened her wings and put one on the shoreline. Haggis led the others onto the wing. After a bit of a climb the three friends were high on Nessie's back. They sat themselves down between her two horns at the back of her head. 'OK,' shouted Haggis, 'ready when you are, Nessie.' With that she spread her wings and with one enormous flap she rose from the loch into the air above the water. Tilting slightly to turn she lined herself up with the horizon and started to fly down the loch. Ben, Louis and Haggis held on tight as the wind blew through their ears.

'Wooow,' shouted Louis, 'this is awesome!' All of them were smiling with the excitement of flying as Nessie raced on down the loch. Suddenly, and without warning, she swooped to the left in a huge turn that pointed her back the way they'd come. Far in the distance they could see Haggis's castle. It looked like a tiny dot on the shoreline so far away. 'Off we go again!' shouted Haggis, as Nessie speeded up back towards the castle.

Before they knew it they were back. Nessie came in for a gentle landing. After all, she couldn't afford for her little friends to fall off into the loch. Nessie spread her wing out to the shoreline once more; the three friends climbed down and made their way back to solid ground.

'Thanks, Nessie,' said Ben. 'Yes, thanks,' said the others together. Nessie smiled and turned to leave. As she disappeared under the water Haggis said: 'Quick, put your ear in the water and listen.' All three of them knelt down and put their heads in the loch. The sound that filled their ears was like nothing they had heard before. A magical, mystical song. 'That was so beautiful,' said Ben when they had taken their heads out of the water. 'Aye, it is,' said Haggis. 'It's the song Nessie sang the day we met.'

The three friends made their way back up the muddy path towards Haggis's castle. All of them were feeling a little weary from their adventures. 'Would you two like to stay here for the night?' said Haggis. It was beginning to get dark as they arrived back at the castle. 'That would be great, thank you, Haggis,' said Ben.

Ben and Louis settled down by the fire to get warm. Haggis made himself busy preparing fresh mugs of cocoa and putting more shortbread out for everyone to eat. 'Here we are,' said Haggis, handing round the plate of shortbread. 'Help yourselves.' Everyone ate and drank. The conversation soon started and they talked about Nessie. Did Haggis know how old she was? Was she the only one of her kind in the loch? Haggis answered what he could but clearly didn't know everything. 'To be honest, boys, I'm still getting to know the wee lassie,' he said. Their conversation turned to the magic ring and the willow tree it was from. They wondered where the tree might be and whether they would ever see it. 'I'm just grateful we have this ring,' said Ben. 'It's going to help us have so many adventures together.' Time ticked on and the three little friends became tired. 'Perhaps we should get some sleep,' said Louis. 'Good idea,' said Ben. 'You both OK to sleep here by the fire?' said Haggis. 'Of course we are,' said Ben. The friends said their good nights and curled up to keep warm and sleep.

Chapter 7

A loud 'cock-a-doodle-doo' rang out across the castle grounds, signalling the arrival of a new day. Ben woke with a start. 'You OK?' asked Louis, for he was used to the morning beginning with a cockerel on the farm. 'Yes, I'm fine, just wasn't expecting that,' said Ben. They could hear Haggis in his little kitchen boiling up more hot chocolate and singing to himself. Ben and Louis wandered through to the kitchen and stood in the door listening to their friend. 'What are you singing?' asked Ben. 'Oh,' said Haggis, slightly embarrassed that they were listening. 'I'm trying to teach myself Nessie's song,' he said. 'Ah,' said Louis, 'we thought you must have dropped a pan on your toe, the noise you were making.' Everyone started to laugh. 'You boys are so cheeky,' said Haggis. 'Do you want some breakfast?' 'Yes, please,' said Ben and Louis together.

Once breakfast was cleared away, the three friends left the castle and walked down the muddy path towards the loch. 'So are you boys heading back to the farm?' asked Haggis. 'Yes,' said Louis, 'Mikey will be wondering where we are.' 'Haggis, would you like us to come and collect you, the next time we use the magic ring for an adventure?' asked Ben. 'Aye, laddie,' replied Haggis, 'I most certainly would.' 'Sounds like a great idea,' said Louis. 'We could have a big adventure together.'

'Right, you'd better show me how this thing works then, hadn't you,' said Haggis. They said their goodbyes, then Haggis stood back to watch the others use the magic ring. Ben and Louis took hold of the ring with both hands. As the ring glowed and their arms began to shake, Ben said: 'Take us to Mikey the shire horse.' With that command they rose from the ground and started to spin around. Their tails were waving and their ears were flapping. Then, without warning, 'pop!' – they disappeared, leaving Haggis standing by the loch looking somewhat stunned. 'Awesome!' he said as he turned and started walking back to his castle.

Seconds later there was another 'pop' and the two mice landed on the ground next to a big hoof. Mikey looked down, somewhat surprised to see his two tiny friends standing there. 'How did you two get here, and where have you been?' Ben and Louis started to explain about the ring, and meeting Wilson the wise owl. They told Mikey about Hamish's kitchen and then arriving at Haggis's castle. Finally they told him about their amazing adventure meeting Nessie and flying down the length of the loch.

'You two come up with some crazy ideas,' said Mikey. 'You don't believe us, do you?' said Louis, sounding very annoyed. 'Nope,' said Mikey. 'Well,' said Ben, 'take a look at this.' He pulled out the magic ring and put both hands on it so that it glowed for a few seconds. Taking one hand off first, he then said: 'Do you believe us now?' 'Wow!' said Mikey. 'Wow indeed,' said Louis, still sounding a little annoyed. 'So can you go to other places with that magic ring?' asked Mikey. 'Yes, we can,' said Ben. 'In that case, you'd better go to the corner of the field where Louis lives, as there is someone waiting there for him,' said Mikey.

The two mice decided to walk across the field, carrying the ring with them. When they arrived in the corner of the field they saw a fluffy bunny rabbit with brown and white patches in her fur. 'Grace!' exclaimed Louis. 'How are you?' 'Worried!' she said. 'I've been worried about you ever since you went into the woods yesterday and then didn't come back last night!' 'Ah yes, sorry about that. We've been on a bit of an adventure,' explained Louis. He introduced his friend to Ben and then explained everything to her. 'That's amazing,' she said. 'I know,' said Louis. 'We are going to go on more adventures soon.' 'Well, if you do, please let me know next time so I'm not sitting here worrying,' said Grace. 'OK,' said Louis. 'I'm off, now I know you're alright,' said Grace. 'I need to teach some baby rabbits how to hop properly.' She turned and with a big hop of her own disappeared into the long grass.

'I guess I should be getting home too,' said Ben. 'Do you have to go?' said Louis. 'I think so, but don't worry, I'll be back soon for a new adventure.' Ben said his goodbyes and started to make his way along the edge of the field. When he reached the farmyard he saw Megan, the farmer's wife, outside washing an empty chicken coop. 'I wonder where the chickens are?' he thought to himself. Being careful not to get soaked or, worse, washed away by the water from Megan's bucket, Ben made his way to the gate. Walking slowly he headed back up the road to the Harwoods' house.

Very cautiously, Ben entered the garden. He had no idea where Hodge the cat was and really didn't want to run into him if possible. Ben had only got about halfway across when the big fat cat jumped down from the garden bin and stood in the middle of the path in front of Ben. 'Oh my,' said Ben, his tiny heart beating ever so fast. Hodge sat down as if in no hurry to move.

Thinking fast, Ben grabbed the magic ring with both hands. As it started to glow he quickly but clearly said: 'Take me to my home in the hole in the wall.' He rose from the ground and span around and around, which Hodge looked totally confused by. Then without warning, 'pop!' – he was gone. The cat just sat there, bewildered at what had happened. Ben, however, was safe and sound back in his little home in the hole in the wall. He placed the ring safely on a shelf and sat down in his chair. 'Phew, that was a close one,' he said.

Later that day Ben was sitting at his table eating his favourite cheese. He'd taken the magic ring off the shelf and placed it on the table. He was taking a close look at it and wondering if there were any other rings like it in the world. Maybe the Golden Willow Tree had left other rings in other places for someone to find. He was still full of the excitement of the last two days and the adventures he'd had. He knew it was nearly bedtime but he wasn't sure if he would be able to sleep. His mind was already thinking of future adventures. Ben took a final sip of hot chocolate before going through to his little bedroom. Climbing into bed and closing his eyes, he was soon asleep. We will have to wait for a new day to find out what adventures it will bring for Ben and his friends.

Ben the Mouse and the Urgle Gurgles

Chapter 1

Ben the mouse lives in a hole in the wall of the Harwoods' kitchen. It's perfect for a mouse, as it's dry and warm. Ben has two friends, Louis and Haggis. Louis is a field mouse, who lives on a nearby farm and Haggis is a hamster, who lives in a castle in Scotland. Our story begins in Ben's home, where he and Louis are doing a little bit of DIY.

Ben was busy tidying some small tools away. 'Nearly done,' said Ben as he raised his head from under the table. 'Can I let go yet?' said Louis. 'Not yet,' said Ben, his head back under the table. 'There we are, all done. You can let go of the table now, Louis, it won't fall over.' 'Finally!' said Louis, sitting himself down in a chair. 'Well, it needed doing,' said Ben. 'That table leg has been very wobbly for a long time. I'm just glad you were here to help me, Louis.' 'My pleasure,' said the little field mouse.

'So,' said Louis, 'any chance of some breakfast?' 'Of course,' said Ben. While Louis sat at the newly repaired table Ben filled a pan with milk and chocolate powder and set it over the fire to boil. He took some cheese from the cabinet and cut it in two. Putting it onto two plates he handed one to Louis. 'There you go, hot chocolate won't be too much longer,' said Ben. 'Thank you,' replied Louis.

The two mice sat drinking their hot chocolate and keeping warm by the fire. Ben's house was perfect for that, as his table and chairs were just close enough to the fire to feel its warmth while eating and drinking. They had been talking about their first adventure with the magic ring and how excited they were to be going on another adventure. 'So we are definitely calling for Haggis first?' asked Louis. 'Yes, definitely,' said Ben. They'd agreed with the Scottish hamster last time they were there that they'd always include him in their adventures. 'Any ideas where we will go this time?' said Louis. 'I have,' said Ben, 'but let's wait and see what Haggis thinks before deciding.' 'Does that mean you're not telling me what they are now?' said Louis. 'Yes, it does,' replied Ben. Louis's face was a picture. He had a real pout on. Ben just laughed. 'You'll know soon enough,' he said. 'Are you finished? We should really get going,' added Ben.

Louis looked up from his hot chocolate, still with a pout on his face. 'Give me a minute,' he said. Ben looked at Louis's hot chocolate and realised he'd not drunk very much. 'You're taking your time this morning,' said Ben. 'Well, if I'm honest, I did have a little breakfast on the farm very early this morning,' said Louis. 'You kept that quiet!' said Ben. Louis smiled; 'You know me, I love my food,' he said. 'Oh, yes,' said Ben, 'I know how much you love your food!'

Chapter 2

The two friends got everything cleared away and took the magic ring down from its shelf. 'We'd best use this outside my little house,' said Ben, as he knew what would happen when they placed their hands on the ring. 'Agreed,' said Louis. 'Let's go into the Harwoods' kitchen, as everyone went out early for their walk today,' said Ben. The two mice stepped cautiously from the mouse hole onto the kitchen floor, always keeping an eye out for Hodge the cat. Wasting no time they both put their little hands on the ring. It started to glow and then to shake their arms up and down. Ben spoke clearly: 'Take us to Haggis the hamster's castle at Loch Ness.' The ring started to spin, lifting them from the floor. At that moment Hodge the cat came through the cat flap. He stopped dead in his tracks. Staring ahead of him he could see not one, but two mice, spinning in the air. He got himself ready to pounce, but he was too late. With a loud 'pop' the mice disappeared, leaving Hodge standing in the middle of the kitchen looking very confused.

Seconds later Ben and Louis were standing outside Haggis's castle, by Loch Ness. 'That was close!' said Louis. 'Yes, and not the first time the ring has saved me from that cat!' said Ben. Louis knocked on the tiny castle door. I should explain that this castle has a normal castle door and gate for people to use. It also has a special tiny door just for Haggis. 'There's no answer,' said Louis. 'That's strange,' replied Ben. They tried again, and then again a few minutes later.

'Well, he's clearly not in. I wonder if he's out on the loch with Nessie,' said Ben.

The two mice made their way from the castle to the edge of the loch along the muddy path. When they arrived at the water's edge they could see no sign of Haggis or Nessie. 'Perhaps they're at the other end of the loch,' said Louis. 'We won't be able to see from here,' said Ben. 'We need to get high up so we can see more of the loch.' 'Let's ask the ring to take us to the top of that mountain,' said Louis, pointing to a snowy peak high above them. 'Good idea,' replied Ben.

Taking out the ring, they each held it with both of their hands. The ring began to glow and as their little arms started to shake, Ben spoke very clearly, saying: 'Take us to the top of that mountain.' He looked at where he wanted to go and the ring must have known. A few seconds later they were spinning in the air with their feet and tails waving and their ears flapping. All of a sudden, and without any warning, 'pop' – they disappeared and reappeared high on the mountainside. 'Louis,' said Ben, 'I think the ring must know we are mice because it's put us down just below the snowy part of the mountain.' 'Good thing,' said Louis, 'I've not got any winter clothes with me.' 'Let's go over there and get a better view of the loch,' said Ben, pointing off towards the right.

The two mice started walking towards a rocky outcrop. They could see much of the loch, but from the rocks they'd be able to see the whole thing, and hopefully Haggis and Nessie too. Finally, and after a great deal of effort, they reached the rocks. 'How are we going to climb these?' said Louis. 'Carefully,' said Ben with a smile on his face. 'I'm serious!'

exclaimed Louis. 'I know,' said Ben, 'just follow me.' With that he started to climb, following a crack in the rock that led to the top. Louis carefully followed behind him, placing his paws in the same spots to make sure he didn't fall. After what seemed like a long time the two arrived on top. The view stretched out for miles in every direction. 'Wow!' said Louis, 'What an amazing view.' He was right, it was amazing. All around them were snow-capped mountains, with green and purple thistles below the snow line. The air was clear and very cold; the sky a crystal-clear blue. 'I think I finally understand why Haggis loves to live in this remote part of the world,' said Ben: 'It is beautiful.'

Just as he said this a warm, wet and slightly smelly air brushed past his ears. There was something, or someone, behind them! Both Louis and Ben span round on their feet to face the mountain. There, standing only a few feet away, was an enormous mountain wolf! It had a coat of long grey, white and brown fur, as well as sharp pointed ears and a bushy tail – none of which the mice had noticed, as they were far more concerned with its large teeth!

'Well, well, well,' said the wolf. 'Fancy finding you two so far up the mountain! I was just thinking to myself it's almost time for lunch!' With that he gave a big grin that revealed even more teeth. 'We're done for!' said Louis. The wolf lowered his back legs ready to pounce. He opened his mouth as wide as he could and jumped.

Ben and Louis closed their eyes; with no time to use the ring there was nothing else they could do. They felt themselves being picked up, but instead of the warm wetness of the wolf's mouth, they felt the cold of the mountain air blowing through their ears. Ben opened his eyes, almost too scared to look. There above him was Haggis riding on Nessie's head. He and Louis were safe in her giant claws. Far below them on the rocky outcrop lay the unconscious wolf, who Nessie had knocked out of the way in her daring rescue of the two mice.

Chapter 3

Nessie came into land at the water's edge. Carefully placing the mice on the shore, she lowered her wing so Haggis could climb down and join his friends. 'What were you two doing all the way up there?' said Haggis. 'Trying to get a good view to find you and Nessie,' replied Ben. 'How did you know we were up there?' asked Louis. 'Och, that was wee Nessie, she's got very good hearing and heard the ring pop as you landed,' said Haggis. 'We knew it was only a matter of time before that evil wolf found you, so we headed your way as fast as we could.' 'Well, we're glad you did,' said Ben. 'Thank you, Nessie,' he said turning to her. She smiled, then turned round and headed off into the deep waters of the loch, leaving the three friends on the shore.

They made their way back up the muddy path to Haggis's castle, where he served them hot cocoa. 'I take it you're here for an adventure?' said Haggis. 'We are,' said Ben, 'although I think we just had one!' They all started to laugh, but deep inside they were all grateful for Nessie's amazing hearing and the rescue. 'So,' said Louis, 'what's the plan?' 'The plan,' said Ben, 'is to try something new.' 'What do you mean?' said Haggis. 'I mean, let the ring take us somewhere we've never been, where no one has ever been!' said Ben. 'Hold on a minute!' said Louis, sounding a little worried. 'This sounds very dangerous.' 'Don't worry, Louis, we will ask the ring to take us somewhere safe,' said Ben.

The three friends cleared away the cups from their cocoa and made their way outside the castle. 'OK, let's all hold the magic ring,' said Ben. As they all placed their hands on the ring it began to glow. Their arms started to shake up and down. Ben spoke clearly, saying: 'Take us to a safe place no one has ever been before.' The ring lifted them off the ground and they started to spin around and around. Then, without any warning, 'pop' – they disappeared.

Seconds later they were standing in a strange magical land full of bright colours. 'Where are we?' asked Haggis. 'No idea,' said Louis. 'Let's take a look around,' suggested Ben. They started to walk around. The place was full of bright, colourful trees and plants. As they took a closer look they realised something very strange. All the trees and plants, in fact everything around them, was made of sweets! 'Have you seen this?' said Haggis, picking up a flower and taking a bite. 'Yum,' he said, 'toffee flavour.' 'This place is amazing,' said Louis. 'Everything here is made of sweets and candy.'

As the three friends walked along a path made of light-yellow toffee they started to ask themselves if there was anyone living here. Then before they could even answer their own questions a little colourful, but hairy, figure appeared. He was slightly taller than Haggis, with green and pink hair all over him from head to toe. His little bare feet were sticking out from below his long hair and a big pink nose appeared in the middle of his face, surrounded by yet more hair. 'Hello,' he said, 'welcome to the land of the Urgle Gurgles.'

Chapter 4

'The land of what?' said Louis, loudly and without thinking. 'Urgle Gurgles,' said the hairy creature. 'And who are the Urgle Gurgles?' asked Ben, somewhat more politely than Louis. 'Us,' said lots of voices at once. Within minutes the three friends were surrounded by little hairy creatures of various colours: green and pink, yellow and pink, blue and pink, even purple and pink. 'Do you all live here?' said Haggis. He kind of knew the answer already, but felt he should say something. 'Yes,' said the first Urgle Gurgle to speak to them, 'we do, and you are most welcome here.' 'Thank you,' said Ben; 'We're excited to be here.'

The Urgle Gurgle spoke again. 'My name is Fuzzy Gurgle. What are your names?' 'This is Haggis,' said Ben, pointing at Haggis, 'and this is Louis,' said Ben, doing the same, 'and I'm Ben.' 'What are you?' said Fuzzy Gurgle. 'Ben and I are mice, and Haggis is a hamster,' said Louis. 'Where are you from?' said Fuzzy Gurgle, 'Because you're clearly not from around here.' 'We live in a place called Lichfield,' said Ben. 'Well, Louis and I do; Haggis is from Loch Ness in Scotland.' 'Never heard of them!' said Fuzzy Gurgle. 'Well, I think they are very far away,' said Ben. Ben explained how they travelled using the magic ring, which all the Urgle Gurgles seemed very impressed with.

'Well,' said Fuzzy Gurgle, 'you are most welcome here in the land of the Urgle Gurgles. You must come to our great hall and join us for lunch.' 'Count us in!' said Louis. Although he was the smallest of the three friends, he was always the hungriest. Any chance for food and he'd take it. Ben and Haggis just smiled at each other, as they knew their little friend well. 'Follow me,' said Fuzzy Gurgle, as he led them and the other Urgle Gurgles along the path and through the trees to the great hall.

The hall itself towered over them all. It looked as if it was made of a giant chocolate cake. Louis's mouth was watering, just looking at it! Surrounding the hall were more trees. They looked similar to the ones they'd just passed. Their trunks were like giant sticks of rock – the kind you'd buy at the seaside. At the top of the trees were huge balls of candy floss, but it wasn't pink; it was various shades of green and yellow. 'Come on in,' said Fuzzy Gurgle as he pushed open the door to the great hall.

As they stepped through the doorway into the great hall the three friends couldn't believe their eyes! As if the world outside hadn't been enough, in the great hall they were greeted with a wondrous, magical sight. There were sweets hanging from the ceiling and glowing, like lights. They looked like giant candy chandeliers. There was a long table that stretched the length of the hall. On either side of it were place settings, with sweets piled high all the way down the middle. 'Come in, come in,' said Fuzzy Gurgle. 'Take a seat.'

The three friends sat together with Fuzzy Gurgle and some of his friends. 'Help yourselves,' he said to them. As everyone tucked into chocolates, toffees, fudge and every kind of sweet you can imagine, the conversation started up again. 'So,' said Fuzzy Gurgle, 'is your home like this?' 'Och, no, laddie,' said Haggis, 'it's very different where we come from.' 'Different, how?' said Fuzzy Gurgle. 'Well, for a start not everything is made of sweets,' said Ben. 'Really?!' said Fuzzy Gurgle, sounding surprised. 'Then what do you do for food?' 'We eat cheese, and vegetables like carrots,' said Louis, smiling at Fuzzy Gurgle. 'Oh my!' said Fuzzy Gurgle, taking a closer look at Louis's smile. 'How did you manage to have such a good set of teeth?' 'What do you mean?' said Louis.

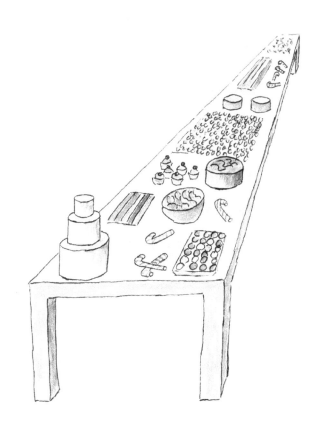

Fuzzy Gurgle opened his mouth to show the three friends his teeth – well, what was left of them, for there weren't many. 'Crikey!' said Louis. 'Och, no, laddie, what happened to your teeth?' said Haggis. 'It's the sweets,' said Fuzzy Gurgle. 'It's all we have to eat, but it's ruining our teeth.' 'Hmm,' said Ben, thinking for a moment. 'Perhaps we can help.' 'How?' said Louis, Haggis and Fuzzy Gurgle all at the same time. 'The farm!' said Ben. 'We could ask Sam, the farmer, for some vegetables for the Urgle Gurgles.' 'Great idea,' said Haggis, 'with just one small problem. How are we going to get them here?'

Louis stood up from his seat and started to pace up and down. He could always think better when he was walking around. 'Aha!' he said very loudly, making everyone jump. 'I've got it!' 'Go on then, laddie, spill the beans, tell us what the answer is,' said Haggis. 'Seeds!' said Louis. 'We will ask Sam for seeds and the Urgle Gurgles can grow all the vegetables they need!' 'Brilliant!' said Ben.

Chapter 5

Getting up from the table to join Louis, Ben started to talk through what they needed to do. Everyone agreed the best thing would be to take Fuzzy Gurgle back to the farm with them to meet Sam the farmer. After lunch Fuzzy Gurgle sat down with the other Urgle Gurgles to discuss the offer made by the three friends. The Urgle Gurgles were a bit worried their friend might not return from this daring adventure. However, they agreed that something had to be done before all the teeth in the land were lost forever!

Stepping outside the great hall, Ben, Louis, Haggis and Fuzzy Gurgle stood round the magic ring. Ben explained that, no matter what happened, Fuzzy Gurgle must not let go. Picking it up and all holding it with both hands, they saw the ring begin to glow. As their arms started to shake Ben said very clearly: 'Take us to the kitchen table in Sam the farmer's house.' With that the ring lifted the four of them off the ground and started to spin them around, their little feet flying out behind them. Suddenly, and without warning, there was a loud 'pop' and the four of them disappeared, leaving the other Urgle Gurgles standing there looking completely stunned.

A few seconds later, another 'pop', and they were standing in the middle of the kitchen table in the farmhouse. Megan, the farmer's wife, was at the sink, looking out across the field where Louis lived. She span round to find the four of them on her table. 'Well, hello,' she said, 'what are you all doing putting paw prints on my nice table?' 'Oh, sorry,' said Louis, 'we just need to talk to Sam if he's around.' 'That's

OK, Louis,' said Megan. 'Give me a minute and I'll go and find him.' She left the kitchen and the four of them made themselves comfortable by sitting down on the table top.

A few minutes later Sam, the farmer, walked in with Megan right behind him. They both sat down on chairs at the kitchen table to listen to what Louis had to say. It took him some time to explain about the ring and the adventures he and Ben had been on. Most grown-ups might not have believed them, but Sam and Megan were different. They always listened to their animals and showed a real interest in their stories. Besides, with Fuzzy Gurgle sitting on their table, there was no denying that this story was very real.

'Please may I take a look at your teeth?' said Megan to Fuzzy Gurgle. He opened his little mouth and both Megan and Sam looked in. 'Oh, my,' she said. 'Hmm,' said Sam, 'we definitely need to do something about this.' 'Are all the Urgle Gurgles the same?' asked Megan. 'They are,' said Fuzzy Gurgle, with a sadness in his voice. Sam turned to Ben and

Louis: 'And you two think some vegetables could help?' he said. 'We do,' said Ben and Louis together. 'If the Urgle Gurgles changed their diet from just sweets, their teeth would have a chance of staying strong,' said Ben. 'They're right, you know,' said Megan to her husband. 'I know,' he replied. 'Give me a minute,' he said to them all. He got up from the table and left the room.

When he returned he was carrying a tiny packet of seeds, small enough for a mouse to lift. 'Here,' he said. 'I've put in some carrot, potato, cabbage, broccoli and cauliflower seeds. That should be enough to get you started. Louis will show you how to plant them, he's seen me do it often enough.' 'Thank you so much,' said Fuzzy Gurgle. 'You may have just saved all the teeth in the land of the Urgle Gurgles.' Megan and Sam smiled. 'It's our pleasure,' Megan said. 'Now,' said Sam, 'are you four going to show us how this magic ring works?' 'Yes!' said Louis, jumping to his feet.

The four of them stood round the ring, just as they had before. Sam had strapped the seeds to Fuzzy Gurgle with some string, so his hands were free to hold the ring. The farmer and his wife watched in amazement as the four of them rose from the table and span around. Then, without warning, 'pop' – they disappeared, arriving back outside the great hall in the land of the Urgle Gurgles. Ben had given clear instructions to the ring to place them there, as all the Urgle Gurgles would be waiting for them.

Chapter 6

'Pop' went the ring, making all the Urgle Gurgles jump. They were very pleased to see their friend, Fuzzy Gurgle, return safely. 'What are those things you're carrying?' a number of the Urgle Gurgles asked Fuzzy Gurgle. 'Vegetable seeds,' said Fuzzy Gurgle, 'and Louis is going to show us how to plant them.' Everyone seemed very excited, if somewhat confused, by this news. For none of them had ever seen a vegetable before or indeed ever planted a seed.

Louis looked around him. 'I think we have a problem,' he said to Ben and Haggis. 'I can't see any mud to put the seeds in.' 'Och, no!' said Haggis; 'You're right. Everywhere is made of sweets. Vegetables won't grow in sweets!' Fuzzy Gurgle had overheard them. 'I think I know a way round that,' he said. 'Come with me.' So the three friends, once again, followed Fuzzy Gurgle through the trees. When they emerged they saw before them a strange red patch on the ground. 'I think they might grow in this,' said Fuzzy Gurgle. 'It isn't made of sweets.' Louis bent down to take a closer look. The red patch on the ground seemed to be hard and soft and wet all at the same time. A bit like a water melon.

'Pass me a seed, please,' said Louis. Fuzzy Gurgle took the seed packet off his back, pulled out a long stripy seed and handed it to Louis. 'Right,' said Louis, 'this is what you need to do.' He bent back down and pulled some of the red ground to one side and put the seed in the hole. Covering it again, he patted it down and stood up. 'What happens next?' said Fuzzy Gurgle. 'Oh, you'll have to wait a few weeks for the vegetables to grow,' said Louis. But everyone was busy watching the red patch of ground behind Louis. Louis noticed they weren't listening and turned to see what was going on. To his absolute amazement there, standing in the red ground, was a fully grown carrot. 'Wow,' said Louis. 'I've never seen one grow that fast before!'

Ben, Haggis and Louis got to work, helping the Urgle Gurgles plant all the seeds that Sam the farmer had given them. Within minutes the Urgle Gurgles had a full crop of vegetables to harvest. At one end of the magic red patch Louis and the Urgle Gurgles were putting seeds in the ground. At the other end Ben was helping Haggis dig up the vegetables ready for eating.

'I guess we'd better show these guys how to cook the vegetables,' said Ben. 'Good idea,' said Louis. 'Perhaps we could make vegetable soup,' suggested Haggis. 'It will make the vegetables go further.' 'Great,' said Ben. 'I'll try and find Fuzzy Gurgle and show him what to do.'

After much work everyone sat down in the great hall once again for food. But this time on the menu was vegetable soup instead of sweets. Most of the Urgle Gurgles seemed to enjoy the soup. There were a few who wanted sweets instead. But when Fuzzy Gurgle explained that the vegetables were good for their teeth they soon ate what was in front of them.

After dinner Ben, Louis and Haggis sat and listened to stories about the land of the Urgle Gurgles. It was Haggis who pointed out that it was getting very late. 'We should be making our way home, boys,' he said. 'You're right,' said Ben. They all said their goodbyes to Fuzzy Gurgle and his friends and got the magic ring out ready to travel home.

Chapter 7

Standing round the ring, Ben, Louis and Haggis placed their hands on it and it started to glow. As their arms began to shake up and down Ben spoke clearly: 'Take us to Haggis's castle at Loch Ness,' he said. The ring span, lifting them off the ground. The Urgle Gurgles stood watching as – 'pop' – their new friends disappeared. A few seconds later the three friends were standing outside the small door to Haggis's castle.

'Would you two like to come in?' said Haggis. 'If you don't mind, Haggis, I think we'd better be heading home, as it is starting to get dark,' said Ben. 'Och aye,' said Haggis, and with that he went inside his castle. 'Let's get you home next,' said Ben to Louis. 'OK,' said Louis, placing his hands back on the magic ring. Ben placed his hands on the ring too and it started to glow again. A few moments later, after the usual shaking and spinning, the two mice appeared with a 'pop' in the corner of the field where Louis lived.

'Where have you two been this time?' came a voice from the long grass. 'Hello, Grace,' said Louis. At that moment a brown and white bunny appeared. 'Hello,' she said. Ben and Louis told her about their adventures. About their run-in with the wolf and how Nessie had rescued them. Then all about the land of the Urgle Gurgles and how Sam the farmer had helped them with vegetable seeds. 'You two have some great adventures,' said Grace. 'I'd love to stay longer, but I've got to get all the baby bunnies to bed,' she said, turning and hopping off into the long grass. 'Talking of bed,' said Ben, 'I should really be getting back home to mine. I'll see you tomorrow.' 'Will do,' said Louis.

Ben held the ring one last time. As it glowed and his arms shook he said: 'Take me to my home in the hole in the wall.' His feet lifted from the ground and he span round and round. Then 'pop' – he disappeared, leaving Louis in the field alone. Seconds later Ben was back in his little home. He put the magic ring safely on its shelf and made himself a hot chocolate. He sat by his fire for a while wondering if he would see Fuzzy Gurgle again. Once his hot chocolate was finished he got ready for bed. He made sure he brushed his teeth, especially after the adventure they'd had that day. Then he climbed into bed and was soon fast asleep.

Ben the Mouse and the Boat Race

Chapter 1

Ben the mouse lives in a hole in the wall of the Harwoods' kitchen. The Harwoods are an elderly couple in Lichfield and their bungalow is close to a local farm. Ben's best friend, Louis the field mouse, lives on the farm and that's where our adventure begins today.

'Morning, Louis,' said Ben as he walked through the mud at the edge of the farmer's field. 'Morning,' shouted Louis from the top of a tall stem of wheat. 'What are you doing up there?' said Ben. 'Just looking around to see if Grace the bunny rabbit is up and about,' said Louis. 'Can you see her?' said Ben. 'I'm not too sure,' said Louis, 'there's some long ears in the next field among the corn.' 'That will be her,' said Ben. 'She's probably setting up for her baby bunny hopping lessons. Why do you want to see her?'

Louis climbed down the stem of wheat he was sitting on. 'Oh, I was hoping she'd be free to join us later at the pond.' 'What's going on at the pond?' asked Ben. 'Our next adventure!' exclaimed Louis, with a big smile on his face. 'What do you mean?' said Ben. 'You'll have to wait and see,' replied Louis. 'It's a surprise!' 'OK,' said Ben, 'I love surprises.'

'We'd better head up to Scotland and find Haggis if we are having an adventure,' said Ben. 'You know how much he enjoys coming along.' 'You're right,' said Louis. 'I'll catch up with Grace later on. Let's get going.' Ben took out the magic ring. Just as they had done so many times before, they both placed their hands on the ring. It started to glow and their arms began to shake up and down. Then speaking clearly Ben said: 'Take us to Haggis's castle at Loch Ness.' The ring lifted them from the ground and started to spin. Ben's and Louis's ears were flapping and their feet and tails flew out behind them. Then suddenly, 'pop' – they disappeared from the corner of the field. Grace's ears stood up as she'd heard the popping sound. 'Those boys are off somewhere again!' she said to her class of baby bunnies.

Chapter 2

A few seconds later they were standing outside the little door in the side of Haggis's castle. Louis gave the knocker a loud bang. 'Hopefully he's in this time. I don't fancy another run-in with that wolf!' said Louis. 'Me neither,' said Ben. Just then the door creaked open and standing there in his fine Scottish tartan was Haggis. 'Hello there, boys!' he said. 'What brings you to these wee parts?'

'We're here to invite you on an adventure,' said Ben. 'Great!' said Haggis; 'Well, don't just stand there, come on in.' Ben and Louis made their way into the castle. They followed Haggis to his little fireplace and sat down on the rug next to it. 'Would you boys like a wee cocoa, before we start?' said Haggis. 'Yes, please,' said Ben and Louis. Haggis made himself busy in the kitchen preparing the cocoa. A few minutes later he brought through three little cups of cocoa. 'Here you are, boys,' he said, 'drink up.' Everyone sat by the fire drinking their cocoa. 'So what's the plan?' said Haggis to Ben. 'Oh, don't look at me,' replied Ben. 'Louis has a surprise for us back at his farm.' 'Sounds exciting,' said Haggis. 'Before we go, would you like to say hello to Nessie?' 'Yes, most definitely,' said Ben. 'Absolutely,' said Louis. All three friends had grown very fond of the big monster from the loch. They'd not met any other monsters, but all agreed she was probably the friendliest one they were ever likely to come across.

When all the cocoa was finished, and cleared away, Ben, Louis and Haggis left the comfort of the castle and made their way down the muddy path that led to the loch. Haggis had brought his magic horn with him, which he used to call Nessie. When they arrived at the water's edge Haggis blew the horn. It made a strange, eerie sound, like the one you get as bagpipes are warming up before they start playing properly. Then, in the distance, they could see her: a huge, green, scaly monster gliding effortlessly through the waters of the loch in their direction.

'What's she pushing?' asked Louis. 'I don't know,' said Ben. In front of Nessie was an object in the water. She was pushing it with her nose. She got closer and closer as the three friends watched. Then finally it was Haggis who spoke. 'She's got a wee boat with her; look, boys, can you see it?' 'We can,' said Ben. A few moments later Nessie arrived at the shoreline, slowing down as she approached with her little boat in front of her. 'Wow,' said Louis, 'it really is a wee boat.'

The three friends took a close look. The boat was tiny, far too small for a person like you or me to fit in. But it was just big enough for two mice and a hamster. The boat was made of wood, and in its middle there was a small mast with a sail attached. There were three seats in the boat: one at the front, one at the back and one in the middle, by the mast. 'Is this for us?' asked Haggis. Nessie nodded. 'Och, thank you, lassie,' he said. 'Where did you get it?' asked Ben. Nessie just smiled and looked down the loch, as if to indicate it had come from far away. 'Well,' said Louis, 'thank you, Nessie.' She smiled again and then sat back in the water and looked at them.

'I think she wants us to try it out,' said Ben. 'But none of us can sail!' said Louis. 'Aye, true,' said Haggis. He turned to Nessie and said: 'Will you teach us, lassie?' Nessie nodded again. So the three friends climbed into the boat. Louis sat at the front, Ben in the middle by the mast and Haggis at the back. There he found a little rudder to steer with. They pushed the boat away from the shore into the open water of the loch. Nessie was looking at Ben. 'I think she wants you to hoist that sail,' said Haggis. 'OK,' said Ben, pulling hard on the little rope next to him. Slowly the sail rose to the top of the mast. Ben tied the rope at the bottom of the mast. 'There we go,' he said, 'ready to set off now.'

The three friends looked up at Nessie. She smiled and with the most gentle of blows from her nostrils she filled the sail and they started to move over the waters of the loch. All three of them could feel the air rushing past their ears as they glided along. Nessie swam alongside her three friends, keeping a close eye on them. Haggis had taken hold of the rudder and was helping to keep their course straight as they journeyed across the loch. 'This is awesome!' shouted Louis. 'Thank you, Nessie!'

As they approached the end of the loch, Nessie looked at Haggis. 'Oh, aye, girl,' he said as he pulled the rudder towards him, making the little boat turn in a big arc across the water. As soon as they were facing the other way he straightened the rudder up and Nessie gave them a gentle blow in the direction of Haggis's castle. Once again the three friends could feel the air rush past their ears as they headed home.

It wasn't long before they were back at the shoreline with Nessie lying in the shallow water next to them. 'That was great fun,' said Ben. 'And it's not over!' said Louis. 'What do you mean?' asked Ben and Haggis together. 'Well,' said Louis, 'I may as well tell you the surprise I had for you, as it looks like Nessie had a similar one planned.' 'Go on, laddie,' said Haggis. 'Back at the farm I'd made arrangements for all three of us to be part of a boat race at the pond,' said Louis. 'I spoke to Mr Drake yesterday and he said he'd love us to join in.' 'Who is Mr Drake?' asked Haggis. 'He's a duck who lives on the pond with his family,' said Louis. 'Well,' said Ben, 'I definitely feel ready for a boat race after Nessie's lesson today.'

Chapter 3

'I've got an idea,' said Ben. 'Let's take our boat to the pond!' The others looked at him. They were both wondering how two little mice and a hamster could move a wooden boat halfway across the country. Even with the magic ring it was impossible. The most they'd ever transported with the ring was a packet of seeds for Fuzzy Gurgle. 'I know what you're both thinking,' said Ben, 'and you're right: it's not possible even with the magic ring. But you've forgotten one thing.' 'What's that?' said Louis and Haggis together. 'Nessie!' said Ben.

'What do you mean?' asked Louis. 'Think about it,' said Ben. 'She could fly us and the boat to the pond at the farm. No one would see her and she could meet everyone at the pond!' 'Wow,' said Haggis, 'that would be an adventure alright!' He turned to Nessie: 'What do you think, lassie, would you like to come?' Nessie sat up in the water, having listened to the conversation. She looked at the three friends, smiled and nodded. 'Awesome!' said Louis. 'Everyone would love to meet you.'

Ben, Haggis and Louis sat together for a while working out the best way to do this epic journey. They knew which direction to travel in but weren't sure how to find the farm, as none of them had ever been in the sky above it before. 'So how will we know we've got there?' asked Ben. Louis stood up and started to pace up and down. He always did this when he was thinking. 'I've got it!' he announced. 'Go on, then, tell us,' said Ben. 'Mikey, the shire horse,' said Louis. 'He's always in the middle of the field, so if we fly low enough we will be able to see him and find our way.' 'Perfect!' said Haggis.

They decided the best way to travel would be in the boat. Nessie could carry the boat, and the three friends could sit on board, giving directions when needed. 'Let's get going,' said Ben as he climbed into the boat. Louis and Haggis followed, taking the same seats as before. Nessie stood up on her back legs. She was enormous! She leant forward and picked up the boat in her claws. Holding it very carefully she opened her wings and took to the air. The three friends grabbed on to the sides of the boat to steady themselves as they went high into the sky.

Nessie turned and started to fly south. At first she had to fly quite high in the sky to clear the mountains that surrounded her loch and others in the Scottish highlands. Ben, Louis and Haggis looked out from their wooden boat, safe in Nessie's grip. They watched as they flew past eagles and hawks and other birds. 'This is amazing,' thought Ben. Slowly Nessie reduced her altitude and began to fly at a lower level, and they crossed the border into England. They could see the remains of Hadrian's Wall below them. This was an adventure like no other. A boat flying in the arms of a monster, and no one could see them except other birds and animals.

'There!' shouted Louis, pointing down at a field far below them. Nessie turned and swooped back, much lower this time so they could get a second look. 'That's definitely Mikey,' said Louis, 'and look – there's the pond!' 'OK,' said Ben, 'let's head for the pond, then.' With that Nessie slowed down and made her final approach. She came into land at the edge of the woods near the pond. However, her landing wasn't as quiet as they'd hoped. With an enormous thud, her back legs crashed onto the ground, making the twigs and leaves around them fly up into the air. The thud was so loud that it made the pigs in the farmyard jump. Mikey stopped eating his hay to see what had happened. Even Wilson, the wise owl, deep in the woods was woken from his lunchtime nap by the noise.

Everyone at the pond turned to see what was going on. Grace was there with her class of baby bunnies. The Drake family all looked up to see Nessie sitting there, still holding the little boat containing Ben, Louis and Haggis. 'Oh, my!' said Grace, looking up at Nessie. The baby bunnies all ran over to her. Mr Drake waddled towards Nessie. 'Hello there,' he said. Nessie smiled and gently placed the wooden boat on the ground. Ben, Louis and Haggis jumped out. 'Hello,' said Louis, 'I hope we're not too late for the boat race.' Mr Drake looked at Nessie, then at Ben and Haggis. Finally he looked at Louis and said: 'Well, you boys certainly know how to make an entrance, and no, you've not missed the race.' He then asked: 'Who might this be?' looking back up at Nessie.

'This is Nessie, from Loch Ness in Scotland, where I live,' said Haggis. 'She brought us here because she wanted to meet you all,' he went on. 'Also she provided this boat for me, Ben and Louis.' Mr Drake looked around. Everyone was waiting to see what he would say next. 'Well, Nessie, you are most welcome to visit our pond. I'm sure it's smaller than the loch you're used to.' Just as he finished, Mikey reached the edge of the field and put his head over the fence. 'Hi, everyone, what's all the commotion about?' 'We have a visitor,' said Mr Drake. 'So I see,' said Mikey, looking up at Nessie. 'This is Nessie,' said Louis, jumping up and down so Mikey would see him. 'Ah, yes,' said Mikey, 'you've told me all about her. Nice to meet you, Nessie,' he said.

While Nessie was still smiling, something swooped over her head and landed on the fence next to Mikey. 'Wilson!' shouted Ben and Louis together. 'Hello, everyone,' said Wilson. 'Ah,' he said, 'Nessie from Loch Ness.' He spoke as if he knew her well. 'Do you two know each other?' said Haggis. Nessie nodded. 'Of course we do,' said Wilson. 'We wise owls know all the magical creatures in the land.' 'Amazing,' said Ben. 'So,' said Louis, 'when's this boat race happening, Mr Drake?'

Chapter 4

'Well, let's go to the pond and see if everything is ready,' said Mr Drake. Ben, Louis and Haggis followed Mr Drake as he waddled back towards the pond where Mrs Drake and her three ducklings were waiting. Nessie gently lifted their boat and placed it in the water at the edge of the pond. 'Hello, dear,' said Mrs Drake to her husband. 'Everything is ready. The ducklings have helped set up the race course.' 'Fantastic,' said Mr Drake. 'Now, who wants to take part?'

Ben, Louis and Haggis stepped forward. 'We do!' said Ben. 'Wonderful, anyone else?' said Mr Drake. His three ducklings waddled forward. 'Well, of course,' said Mr Drake, 'I'd expect you three to take part.' Then, to everyone's surprise, Grace hopped forward. 'I'll have a go, if that's OK.' 'Of course,' said Mr Drake. The baby bunnies had a worried look on their little faces. 'Don't worry,' said Grace, 'Mr Drake will look after me.'

'Right, everyone follow me,' said Mr Drake as he waddled over to the edge of the pond. 'If you're taking part, stay with me and if you're watching, please follow Mrs Drake.' Mrs Drake led the spectators round the edge of the pond. Mikey had opened the gate to the field and made his way to the pond. Sam the farmer didn't mind him doing that as he knew Mikey would always come back and close the gate behind him. Nessie lay down on the ground next to the pond. Wilson the owl stood next to her. Then Mikey lay down next to Wilson. The three baby bunnies decided their safest bet was to stay close to

Mikey; they weren't too sure about Wilson and Nessie. Mrs Drake decided she would sit with the baby bunnies too, which put smiles back on their furry little faces.

The end of the pond where the race would begin was a buzz of busyness. Ben, Louis and Haggis were on board their little boat sorting ropes and sails. Mr Drake's three ducklings were each climbing aboard their little boats. Now, I know what you're thinking: ducks don't need boats. However, this was a special event and included animals that couldn't swim, so, to make it fair, all the competitors used boats. The ducklings' boats had holes in the bottom for their webbed feet to go through. This allowed them to paddle along in the water while sitting in a boat like everyone else.

'OK, Grace,' said Mr Drake, 'come this way, I've got a special boat for you.' Grace hopped along behind Mr Drake as he led her to the end of the starting line. There sat a beautiful boat made of twigs and woven with leaves to make it watertight. At the back was a paddle like a wheel. 'Now,' said Mr Drake, 'all you have to do is spin this paddle with your feet and the faster you spin the faster the boat will go.' 'Wonderful, I'm sure I can manage that,' said Grace, gently hopping into the boat and sitting down.

Mr Drake waddled back and on the way checked the three ducklings were ready. Finally he reached Ben and his crew. 'Are you boys ready to race?' he said. 'Yes!' shouted Ben, with a squeak in his voice. 'OK, everyone,' said Mr Drake, 'I'll count to three and quack, then you're off.' Everyone focused on the pond and the course ahead. Quiet fell over the pond as everyone waited, listening carefully for Mr Drake. 'ONE, TWO, THREE, QUACK!' he said as loudly as he could, and with that they were off!

Chapter 5

First off the starting line, which was a surprise to everyone, was Grace. Paddling hard she took the lead. Following close behind were the Drake family ducklings. However, there was one boat that didn't move! Ben, Louis and Haggis hadn't budged an inch. 'What's wrong?' squeaked Louis! 'Och no!' cried Haggis; 'We have nae any wind to blow the sail!' 'This is bad news!' said Ben. Mr Drake overheard them and quacked at Nessie to help. She moved round to where the little wooden boat sat bobbing up and down in the water. Just as she'd done on her loch she gave the sails a gentle blow with her nostrils and finally the three friends set sail. 'Thanks, Nessie,' they squeaked as they set off towards the rest of the competitors.

Ahead of Ben's boat there were problems in the middle of the pond. The youngest of the Drake ducklings had been paddling too hard with his left foot and gone off course and was now stuck in the reeds. He was not a happy duckling. His mum saw how upset he was and left the baby bunnies with Mikey and took to the water to help her duckling. Pulling him from the reeds she said: 'Come with me, little one, and watch from the bank.' The little duckling nodded and followed his mum to the edge of the pond. The baby bunnies helped him out of the boat and he sat with them watching the remaining competitors.

Now the pond had a small island in the middle. It was only the size of a dustbin lid, but it was certainly big enough to be an obstacle in this race. Grace had managed to master the spinning of her paddle and was travelling at a good speed. However, she wasn't so good at the steering, and before she could do anything to stop it, she had crashed into the island.

Mr and Mrs Drake looked at each other and, as if they each knew what the other was thinking, took to flight. They landed at the same time on the island. 'Are you OK, Grace?' asked Mrs Drake. 'Oh, I'm fine, dear, just a little stuck,' said Grace. 'Well,' said Mr Drake, 'I think we will have to tow you to the edge of the pond if that's alright.' 'That's fine,' said Grace, feeling a little embarrassed, but at the same time grateful for the rescue. Mr and Mrs Drake pushed Grace's boat free of the island and then got on either side to steady it as they moved her to the shore. 'OK, you can hop out now,' said Mr Drake. 'Thank you,' said Grace. As she hopped out her three baby bunnies rushed forward to give her a hug. 'I told you I'd be fine, didn't I?' she said, sitting down with them and the others to watch the rest of the race.

There were now just three boats left: the two older Drake ducklings and the three friends in their wooden boat. They were all three-quarters of the way across the pond. Somehow, with their late start, Ben, Louis and Haggis had managed to catch up with the Drake ducklings. This had distracted the oldest ducking. He was watching the wooden boat instead of where he was going. Before he could stop himself he'd crashed into his sister, sending her boat into a spin. Fortunately, his sister managed to keep going, but the oldest duckling was now out of the race.

The final two boats were neck and neck as they approached the finish line. Mr Drake had flown to the end of the pond to make sure all was fair at the finish line. 'QUACK,' he said loudly as the winner crossed the line. 'Who won, who won?' said the baby bunnies to Grace. 'I couldn't tell,' she replied. 'We will have to wait and see,' said Wilson the wise owl.

Everyone got out of their boats and made their way around the edge of the pond to where the spectators were sitting. 'Well,' said Mrs Drake, looking at her husband, 'who won the race?' Mr Drake flew and landed a few feet away on a little rock. From there everyone could see him clearly. 'It is my great pleasure,' he said, 'to announce this year's winners of the annual pond race: Ben, Louis and Haggis!' Everyone cheered! 'Well done, boys,' said Grace. 'Yes, well done,' said Mikey and Wilson. Ben, Louis and Haggis gave hugs to the three ducklings, as shaking hands with a duck is not possible. They also hugged Grace, as she had been their other competitor. 'As a prize,' said Mr Drake, 'Sam the farmer has left you all some cheese and biscuits.' 'Perfect,' said

Louis, thinking about his tummy again. Everyone laughed, as they knew how much he liked his food.

Chapter 6

Sitting down at the edge of the wood, Ben, Louis and Haggis started to eat their cheese and biscuits while Nessie looked on. Mikey, Grace and the baby bunnies had said goodbye and gone back into the field. Just as he always did, Mikey had closed the gate behind him. 'Well, I'm off,' said Wilson the wise owl. 'It was wonderful to see you again,' he said to Nessie, giving a little bow. She smiled at him as he flew off into the dark trees deep in the wood.

Apart from Nessie, it was now just the three friends and the Drake family left. 'Thank you for including us in the race this year,' said Ben. 'Yes, thank you,' said Louis; 'Your ducklings are tough competition,' he added. 'Well,' said Mrs Drake, 'perhaps next year they'll beat you!' 'I don't doubt it,' said Ben. The Drake family said goodbye and waddled off to the pond.

'I guess we should think about making our way back to Scotland,' said Haggis, looking up at Nessie. Nessie nodded. 'Would you like some company on the journey?' said Ben. 'Och aye, yes, laddie,' said Haggis, 'that'd be great.' 'I might head home if you don't mind,' said Louis. 'That's OK,' said Ben, 'I'll go with Haggis and Nessie.' Louis said goodbye and headed off across the field. He stopped on the way to chat to Mikey the shire horse.

'Right, then,' said Haggis. 'I guess we do the same as before.' Ben and Haggis walked round the pond and climbed into the wooden boat, which was still sitting there from the race earlier that afternoon. Nessie carefully lifted the boat out of the water and, with a gentle flap of her wings, launched them all into the air. Mikey and Louis watched them from the middle of the field as they took off into the evening sky.

Nessie turned to point north this time, and set off back towards the Scottish border and then the highlands of home. As they got further north the light began to fade as night arrived and the day was left behind. 'We are going to have to rely on Nessie to find your castle this time,' said Ben. 'Aye,' said Haggis, 'but she flies these skies, so she knows where to go.' 'True,' said Ben. The two of them held on tight and sat enjoying the flight. They could see the lights of the roads and cities below as they passed over them. Slowly even these began to fade as they got further north.

Finally, the only thing below them was the glistening white of the snow-capped mountains. The light of the moon shining in the snow made a magical picture of the land below them. Then, suddenly, Nessie swooped down towards a dark patch between the snowy mountain tops. She had found her loch. 'Look!' said Ben, pointing at a little light. 'My castle!' said Haggis with a smile on his face. Nessie came in for a gentle landing, placing the boat on the waters of the loch right by the shoreline. The two friends climbed out and moored the boat to a rock using the ropes. 'Thank you, Nessie,' said Ben. Nessie smiled and turned. She then dived into the deep waters of the loch. 'I bet she's glad to be home,' said Haggis. 'Coming up to the castle for a cocoa?' he said to Ben. 'That would be great, thanks,' said Ben.

The two friends walked back up the muddy path to the castle and made their way in through the little door. Haggis made some cocoa and got out some shortbread. They sat down by the fire. 'What a day, eh!' said Ben. 'Aye,' said Haggis, taking a huge bite of shortbread and sprinkling crumbs all over his fur. 'It was great fun,' continued Ben. 'We will have to go sailing again sometime.' He took a bite of his shortbread, making a little less mess than his Scottish friend. After a short time they'd finished their cocoa and shortbread.

'Are you heading home tonight?' said Haggis. 'Yes, I think I'd better,' said Ben. 'It's been such a busy day I could do with a good night's sleep in my own bed.' 'Aye,' said Haggis, 'I always sleep better in my own bed too.' Ben got up and said goodbye to his friend and made his way out of the little door in the castle wall. He found some space near the muddy path and took out the magic ring. As he held it with both hands it started to glow, lighting up the ground around him. As his arms began to shake up and down Ben clearly said: 'Take me to the hole in the wall in the Harwoods' kitchen.' With that the ring lifted him, spinning him around and around. Suddenly and without warning, 'pop' – he disappeared.

A few seconds later he was standing in the doorway to his home. He could see Hodge asleep in his basket across the kitchen. He decided not to waste any time getting inside, just in case the fat old cat decided to wake up. Putting the ring on the shelf, he made his way through to his bedroom and got changed for bed. Placing his red jumper in its box he climbed into bed and was soon fast asleep – no doubt dreaming about the adventures he and his friends had been on. As for us, we will have to wait to discover what Ben's next adventure will be!

About the Author

Hi, I'm Andy and this is my first book. I was born in London, but I've lived in the north-west of England for the last 25 years. I'm a dad to Grace and Sam and I used to tell them Ben the mouse stories when they were little. It was Grace who kept encouraging me to write these stories, so you have her to thank for that.

I've had the opportunity to do some amazing things in my life, including working as a prison counsellor in South Africa and teaching blind children to rock climb.

I'm a self-taught artist, which can be a challenge as I have a visual impairment. However, I love being creative, which is why I've enjoyed writing these stories for you. I hope you've enjoyed reading them too. Keep an eye out for more Ben the mouse books. You can follow him at:

www.benthemouse.com

Instagram: @benthemouse